NICE ONE, SAM!

Sam can't believe his luck. After all the waiting he's finally managed to get the sticker he's been dreaming of—Mika Tailer. The best goalie in the world, and Sam's hero.

As soon as the sticker is in Sam's hands it starts to have a strange effect on him. He feels a weird sensation and is filled with a powerful energy—does this mean that Sam might be able to fulfil another of his dreams. Will he make it on to the school football team . . . ?

John Goodwin lives and writes on the Isle of Wight. In addition to his books for children he has written plays for BBC Radio with his daughter, Charlotte. Each year on Boxing Day, John plays goalie in a crazy adults and children's football matc

OTHER OXFORD BOOKS

Mark's Dream Team
Alan MacDonald

The Multi-Million Pound Mascot
Chris Powling

There's Only One Danny Ogle
Helena Pielichaty

Ryan's United
Dennis Hamley

A Game of Two Halves
David Clayton

The Worst Team in the World
Alan MacDonald

The Young Oxford Book of Football Stories
James Riordan

NICE ONE, SAM!

John Goodwin

ILLUSTRATED BY
Clive Goodyer

OXFORD
UNIVERSITY PRESS

OXFORD
UNIVERSITY PRESS

Great Clarendon Street, Oxford OX2 6DP

Oxford University Press is a department of the University of Oxford.
It furthers the University's objective of excellence in research, scholarship,
and education by publishing worldwide in

Oxford New York

Athens Auckland Bangkok Bogotá Buenos Aires Cape Town
Chennai Dar es Salaam Delhi Florence Hong Kong Istanbul Karachi
Kolkata Kuala Lumpur Madrid Melbourne Mexico City Mumbai
Nairobi Paris São Paulo Shanghai Singapore Taipei Tokyo Toronto Warsaw

and associated companies in Berlin Ibadan

Oxford is a registered trade mark of Oxford University Press
in the UK and in certain other countries

British Library Cataloguing in Publication Data available

ISBN 0 19 275182 4

1 3 5 7 9 10 8 6 4 2

Typeset by AFS Image Setters Ltd, Glasgow

Printed in Great Britain by
Cox & Wyman Ltd, Reading, Berkshire

The huge crowd were up on their feet. 'Penalty! Penalty!' they shouted. The referee blew his whistle and pointed to the spot. The crowd cheered and held their arms aloft. Now surely the winning goal would be scored and for their team it would be triumph yet again. Still their cheering echoed round the stadium and mingled with chants of 'Paggio . . . Paggio.'

Roberto Paggio, the team's captain, stepped forward and placed the ball on the spot. The crowd were quiet now and all the players stood quite still. Paggio too stood still. He looked at the ball then at the goal and then back at the ball again. He shook his hands by his sides and then took three very deliberate steps back. All eyes were on the ball . . .

He ran forward swiftly and hit the ball hard and true as only a great player can. The ball was

right on target and zoomed towards the bottom right corner of the net. It was perfection. Yet a blurred low shape was moving to the same spot too. A blurred shape in green was hurling itself towards the ball. Arms were flung forward and in a rolling mass of ball and gloves and goalkeeper's body the penalty was . . .

I switched off the video and dressed for school. Tuesday is 'can't wait' day. It's straight downstairs. Sneak past Mum's and Amber's bedrooms and don't make a sound on the creaking floorboard to wake the dog. Pull the magazine out of the letter box and stuff your fingers in the letter box flap to stop it shutting to with a crash. Then fly upstairs as fast and quietly as you can clutching the magazine tight in your fist. Close your bedroom door without a sound and then breathe more easily. Open the fingers of your hand for your fist full of football fantasy and magic. For Tuesday is the day of *SCORE* and its free football sticker.

Only it wasn't. Not this Tuesday. The letter box was closed with a tight shut mouth. No football magazine sticking out of its jaws. No sticker to add to the collection.

I stared hard at the letter box half expecting the flap mouth to open at any second and the roll of the magazine to be pushed through. I waited for ages. I waited until my toes were blue with cold and my teeth started to chatter.

There was only one thing to do. I'd have to lever open the flap of the letter box, look through it, and see if the magazine was lying outside on the pavement.

But it wasn't. Not this Tuesday. My fingers slipped on the letter box flap and it shut to with a crash. I opened the door as quietly as I could and set off along the pavement faster than the players come out of the tunnel at the start of a match. I had one target in my view—Goodall's

Paper Shop. I began to run. The trees in Lime Grove were the players of the other team. I passed three and they didn't move a centimetre. I was just too quick for their lumbering branches to catch me. The goal was in sight. I went to round a fourth. This was so easy.

Then the defence showed their dirty play. A huge root of a tree viciously burst through a crack in the pavement. It was a brute of a root deep from the black earth. Then it was round my ankle and pulling me crashing to the ground.

'Penalty . . . penalty!' screamed the crowd. Now I was Roberto Paggio and then I was in green and hurling myself sideways along High Street and straight into Goodall's Paper Shop. My gloved goalkeeper hands were ready to grab that fist full of football stickers. Behind the counter stood Mrs Goodall in her referee's black uniform.

'Steady on, lad,' she said, taking a pencil from behind her ear and licking the end of it.

'I want . . . '

'I know what you want,' she said, licking the pencil for a second time. I have

cornflakes for my breakfast and poor old
Mrs Goodall has to make do with a lead
pencil for hers.

'You came in here last week, didn't you?'
she asked as her thick black pencil scrawled
the names of houses onto a huge bundle of
newspapers.

'Yes,' I said quietly.

'Then you'll know the paper boy delivers
your papers.'

'Yes,' I said even quieter.

'So why have you come here?' she asked
lifting an even bigger bundle of newspapers
onto the shop counter. I just stared at the size
of the bundle and no words could find their
way onto my lips.

'I know why,' she said without looking at
me. 'It's those football stickers . . . isn't it?'

I nodded a silent nod.

'And your stickers are in the magazine which
the paper boy has with him.'

It went very quiet in the shop.

'Oh,' I said after a while and took a step back
towards the shop door.

'Lucky I've got a spare packet of them,' said Mrs Goodall as she pulled a set of stickers out of her pocket and threw them towards me. I dived forward and caught them  with the best goalkeeper grip I could manage.

 'For me?' I asked her.

'Well, they're not for Michael Owen. Now take them out of my way. I need to get on with these papers.'

I wanted no second telling and was out of the shop in a stride. Once outside I ripped open the packet of stickers with my teeth. It was a four to one chance. Ben   Buck . . . I'd got him. Vinny Capstick . . . everybody's got him ten times over. Two to go. Please PLEASE! I'll do anything if it could be him. Not be rude to Amber for a whole week . . .

promise . . . promise anything if only . . .
Georgio Fabrizi . . . oh no . . . he's the worst
player ever. And now for the last one. The big
one. I can't look. I won't have . . . him. I know
I won't. Look now.

YES! WOW! YES! YES!

Look again. Pinch yourself. It is

MIKA TAILER

The sticker everybody wants and **nobody**
but **nobody** has got so far. Except me. And
I'm going to keep him. Yes . . . you bet I am.
Never take my eyes off him. **Mika** the best
goalkeeper of all time. **Mika** the greatest
footballer ever. **Mika** the only goalkeeper to
save three penalties in a world cup final.
Mika my hero.

I just stood and stared at his face. I had been
trying to collect his sticker ever since the
magazine had first come out and here he was. I
put my finger to the sticker and very carefully

let it go right round the shape of his face. Magic! It was just magic.

My finger was coming back to the top of his head for a second time when it sort of jumped off the sticker. It did it by itself. It was like when you touch something burning hot. But my finger wasn't hot at all. It was cold. I looked at Mika's face again and it seemed to be smiling. I know you might think I was dreaming but I tell you . . . his face was smiling.

I looked at the smiling face for ages. Then my eyes started to go blurry and I couldn't see straight . . . I put the sticker carefully into my big trouser pocket making sure that I didn't crease or crumple it. Very slowly I did up the pocket zip so that it wouldn't rip the sticker. Then I set off home making up my mind that I would run all the way there without stopping.

Smack! A hand grabbed at me. A hand was at my blazer and pulling me back. I was stopped dead in my tracks. I just froze. Then there was laughing. Laughing coming from behind and in front of me. I know that laughing. I'd know it anywhere. Knocker stepped out in front of me from behind the trees in Lime Grove.

'What we got here then? You've got the wrong badge on our blazer, what a shame,' he said with his face very close to mine.

I tried to pull back but Josh still had his hand on my blazer and he wouldn't let go.

'He's a mummy's boy with the wrong badge on his blazer. What a prat,' said Josh.

'Let go,' I said.

'Have you ever seen anybody run like him?' said Knocker. 'He runs like a spider.'

'Please let go . . . ' I said.

'Spider . . . spider,' shouted Josh and Knocker together in a chant.

'He's a spider man,' shouted Knocker louder than ever.

I felt my hand go down towards my trouser pocket. Down towards that sticker. Then I pulled it back sharply.

'Please don't let them find out about that. Anything but that. Don't let them find out about Mika . . . please,' I said to myself.

Then it went very still. Very quiet. Knocker didn't move or say anything. He just stared at me. Josh's hand wasn't pulling at my blazer quite so tight. But I didn't move. I know their tricks. Mean, vicious tricks. The kind of tricks that do your head in and make you feel stupid and scared. Then Knocker said very quietly, 'Where you going, Spider Man?'

I tried to look away from him, to pull my head away from his stare.

'Nowhere,' I said.

'Nowhere?' repeated Knocker and he turned to face Josh. 'There's no such place,' he said. 'I don't know anybody who comes from nowhere

. . . do you, Josh?' Knocker began to laugh again.

'I know what comes from nowhere,' said Josh.

'What's that?' said Knocker.

'Spiders . . . spiders come from nowhere. Smelly little spiders. Nowhere is the only place they can live.'

Now they were both laughing. Rocking about and laughing at their own stupid jokes. I knew I had to make a move. They would only be off guard for a second. It was now or never.

I ducked low. Josh's hand came away from gripping me.

'Watch it. Spider on the loose,' shouted Knocker.

Josh's hand was on my blazer again and pulling it tight. I ducked even lower and strained forward. Still he held on to me. Still I pulled. Now there was a ripping noise. My blazer was ripping. I didn't care. Not one bit. Let it rip all it liked. If it wasn't for stupid blazers none of this would have ever happened in the first place. They'd have had no reason to pick on me. Instead it would have been somebody else.

'Spider spider!' shouted Knocker as he stepped out to block my way. But I started to run. I was like a forward on the wing. I could swerve past him. I knew I could. I kept low to the ground. He lurched at me with both arms outstretched. A giant foul lurch. But I ducked too low for him and then I was past and out into the open spaces of the wide pitch.

'Spider on the loose,' shouted Josh. 'Where are you going? You left half your blazer behind.'

In his fist he had a torn piece of my blazer pocket which he waved in the air. But by now I was over the halfway line and heading for home. Soon the goal would be in sight. When I saw it I dived inside the house and ran straight upstairs to my bedroom. I took off the ripped blazer and stuffed it under the mattress of my bunk bed. It made the mattress a bit lumpy with a bump in the middle. With a few belly flop goalie dives on top of it the lump almost went down to nothing. Unless you looked really close you couldn't tell it was under there at all.

What really mattered was that my trouser pocket was not ripped at all. I undid the zip to see the sticker was still safe and sound. And what's more Mika's face was still smiling at me.

Kick the ball. Kick it hard. Kick it straight. Kick it at the third brick in the wall. Think the brick is Vinny Capstick. Pass it to Vinny with the side of your foot. Don't toe end it. Make it accurate. Vinny passes it straight back. A one–two pass. Control it and then off down the wing. Side step one. Side step two and the goal is in sight. Steady now . . . take aim. Hit the goal below the drainpipe.

Our garden is small. In fact a stamp you post on a letter is bigger than our garden. But it's good for having a kick around. It's got a high fence round it to stop big bullies with giant fists and stupid laughs picking on you.

Now for a bit of heading. Throw the ball up. Just a metre or so. Head straight through the ball. Don't close your eyes. Hit it with your forehead. I hate this bit. Really hate it. The ball

14

seems so hard and I always miss it. Come on
. . . if you are going to be a striker . . . a real
striker, you'll have to learn how to head the
ball. Missed it. I closed my eyes when I
shouldn't have done. Perhaps I am a spider, a
useless hopeless spider just like Knocker says I
am. There to remind me how bad at heading I
was when I didn't need reminding at all was
Tara. She's the girl next door who sometimes
peeps through a little gap in the fence. She
spies on me. I wish she'd got better things to
do.

'Missed it. It's no good closing your eyes like
that. You should have scored from that close,'
she said in that squeaky voice of hers.

I tried to ignore her but still she went on
about it.

'You're scared of it, aren't you? Scared of

heading it. You won't be a real footballer if you can't head it.'

'I can head it, so there.'

'Go on then . . . let's see you.'

I turned my back on Tara's peeping face coming through the gap in the fence and tried to shut her out of my mind. I undid the zip of my trouser pocket. The sticker lay neatly at the bottom of the pocket. It was like the pocket was made for that sticker. It fitted perfectly. I took the sticker out and looked hard at it. It wasn't creased or crumpled or dirty. It was just shiny. I looked hard at Mika's face. 'Come on, Mika,' I said to myself. 'We'll show Miss Squeaky Voice a thing or two.'

My finger was going round the shape of the face without me even having to put it there. For the second time it was coming back to the top of his head when my finger jumped off the picture. It was just like it did before outside Goodall's Paper Shop. Just like before I felt burning hot. Only this time it was my leg that was hot. My right leg was burning. It was burning with Mika power.

Something was guiding my leg towards the football as it lay on the ground. Something was pulling my leg back very slowly indeed. Then forward it went like a rocket. It hit the ball hard and true. *Whack* went the ball straight into the fence and *whack* as it rebounded into the opposite fence. Then the ball took off. Straight into the air it zoomed. *Higher* and *higher* it climbed, heading straight up. I stood and stared at it until it was a tiny dot in the sky. It went out of sight and I thought that was the last time I'd see it. But I was wrong. The tiny dot appeared again but all the time getting bigger. The ball was falling back to earth like a meteorite falling from the sky.

The ball hit the ground at an amazing speed right next to my feet and then went up again. It hit next door's roof and then began to slow down. Now the ball was moving in slow motion back towards our garden. It hovered just above my head and then finally landed into my outstretched hands.

I was gobsmacked. I turned it round slowly making sure it wasn't some alien spacecraft from outer space full of a deadly virus. But it was the same old ball sure enough with scuffed black and white patterns on it. I was still looking at it and up at the sky when I heard that squeaky voice again.

'How did you do that, Sam?' she asked.

'What?' I said.

'That zap kick.'

'Oh that.'

'It was huge.'

'It was nothing,' I said. 'Just my usual skill.'

Football is a tactical game. Keep it tight when you're winning is something you should always remember. So with that in mind I bounced the ball once at my feet and headed for our back door.

Tara shouted, 'That wasn't your usual skill, Sam. Nothing like it. That was just . . . *WOW*!'

I pretended I hadn't heard her. It was time to watch my favourite football video of Mika's famous penalty saves of the World Cup Final. Whilst that was on I was trying to make sense of all that had happened out there in the back garden.

I ran onto the field in a rush. I'd show them this time. I did a spring up and down the pitch before most of the others were out of the changing room. No more miskicking for me. No more feeble tries to head the ball. I was a striker to be reckoned with. A striker that could kick a ball into orbit. I could be in *The Guinness Book of Records*. A famous striker with inter-galactic footballing skills.

Then the rest came out. I heard Josh giggling at me as I ran up and down the touchline but I didn't care. He'd soon see something that would take that stupid grin off his face.

Mr Brailsford gathered us round and picked two teams like he always did.

'Charlton, Wayne, Woody, Daniel, Josh, Edward, and Ben . . . '

Mr Brailsford's picking was just about complete.

'James, Ryan, and . . . Jack.'

There were only two players left in our class without a team. One a giant of a boy with size ten boots and the other a skinny little lad with inter-galactic ambitions.

'Sir . . . what about me?' said the boy with size tens.

'Oh . . . you, Knocker.'

'Yes, sir.'

It went very quiet for a bit and then Mr Brailsford turned to me and Knocker.

'Would you believe it, I almost forgot you two,' he said.

I didn't know what was going on. I thought perhaps we were going to get the red card before we'd even started. Then he said, 'You'll both just have to play in the same team, won't you?'

Knocker glared at me and said, 'Oh, sir . . . can't he play in the other team?'

'No,' said Mr Brailsford. 'I just said you will both play in the same team.'

'But he's useless. A wet wimpy spider with . . . '

But Mr Brailsford didn't let Knocker finish his sentence.

'If I hear another word, Paul, you won't play at all. You can spend the lesson in the changing room. Is that clear?'

Knocker knew it was very clear and that when Mr Brailsford called him Paul and not by his nickname it was serious. Mr Brailsford was a teacher who kept his word.

We kicked off. I positioned myself as a striker and ran up towards the other team's penalty area. I ran fast and hard and found myself with a bit of open space around me. I eyed up their goalie . . . Josh. He wasn't that good. He only went in goal because nobody else in their team wanted to. Surely I could put a shot past him and find the back of the net. All I needed was one good chance. One neat pass from midfield, a quick dart up the pitch and the shot was on. We could be one–nil up, no sweat.

I waited for ages in that open space by myself. Nothing happened. No neat pass came from midfield. No pass came at all. I might as well have been on a different planet for all the part I played in the match. Most of the play happened in the other half of the field and we were soon two–nil down.

When we did get the ball Knocker had it. It was as if it was glued to the end of his size tens and there was nobody else in the team but him. He ran all over the pitch. He barged and pushed, then ran some more, lost control of the ball and shot miles wide of the goal.

Out of nowhere we got a free kick. Mr Brailsford blew his whistle hard.

'Free kick,' he said. 'You take it, Sam. Give it a big kick upfield.' He placed the ball on the ground.

'Not him,' shouted Knocker. 'He can't kick his way out of a bag of chips.'

Some of the kids began to giggle and I could hear Josh far away in the goal with his loud stupid laughing. The more he laughed the worse it was. I felt all stiff in my back just like the time when he grabbed my blazer.

'Don't take any notice of the rest, Sam,' said Mr Brailsford. 'Just give it one big kick.'

I looked at the ball and tried not to think about Knocker or Josh or being a spider. I tried really hard. But somehow I couldn't do it. I couldn't block them out. My foot hit the ground in front of the ball and instead of it flying high up into the air upfield it just trickled forward a few centimetres and then stopped. I could hear booing coming from Josh in goal way upfield. Loud echoing booing.

Mr Brailsford blew his whistle sharply.

'Half time. Change ends . . . and cut out that booing.'

I ran off the field. Not in tears but pretty close to tears and my legs felt all wobbly. I went into the changing room, took something out of my trouser pocket and put it into my football shorts pocket. It would be a risk. It might go very wrong but there was nothing else I could do. I just couldn't stand the thought of that booing happening again.

The second half started. I ran upfield just like before and just like before nobody passed the ball to me. The other team scored and we were three–nil down. It was hopeless. I began to think that run off the field and into the changing room was a complete waste of time. It just didn't seem worth it.

I could feel the sticker that was hidden in my shorts pocket. I traced round where I thought Mika's face would be. I was so busy doing it that I hadn't noticed the ball roll towards me. A perfect pass from midfield. What I'd waited for all game. But I just stood and stared at the ball. Behind me the rest were shouting and yelling. Their cries were getting closer.

'Kick it. Kick it up. Go for goal. Sam, kick it up.'

If I didn't do something soon it would be too late.

I ran forward three steps and looked at the goal. It seemed miles away. Surely I couldn't shoot for goal from this far back. Behind me the rest of the players were so close. The ground was shaking as two size ten boots pounded the turf a few metres away.

It was now or never. I put my hand on the

sticker and felt my leg burn just like before. The burning leg pulled itself slowly back. Too slowly. I could see the studs of Knocker's size tens out of the corner of my eyes. My leg went forward at galactic speed. It struck the ball at seventy miles an hour. Off zoomed the ball goalwards. It didn't head for the stars like last time but was a hard low volley right on target.

Josh saw it coming. He wasn't booing now. No way. That volley had shut him up for sure. He placed himself in the centre of the goal and watched it like a hawk. His hands and body were ready to block its movement when the right moment came. Yet the ball was swerving and gathering speed as it travelled through the air.

Faster and faster it went. I wanted to shout out. To tell everybody that it was impossible to stop a shot like this one. That Josh better move

out of the way before he was killed. Before I could say a word the ball was near the goal and heading for the top corner of the net. Yet it missed the net and crashed into the goalpost. Crunch went the post and down fell the net as the goalpost was broken into two different pieces.

All the players stood on the pitch and looked at the broken mess. Mr Brailsford was leading Josh away from the tangled web of net and post and Josh was scratching his head in a daze. I just stared at it all. Had I done this? Had one kick of the ball caused all this? I couldn't cheer or shout out or say how good it was to hit a shot like that. I should have been dancing round the pitch with my shirt pulled over my head like they do on the telly. Instead I just felt numb. It was like a hurricane had struck.

'What a mess,' said Charlton.

'What a strike,' said Mr Brailsford. 'The strike of the century. I've never seen a kick like it. We shall all have to wear crash hats next. How did you do a kick like that, Sam?'

For some questions it's best not to try and find an answer.

After school I went to the school library for a bit. I wanted to let all the rest of the kids go home before I walked out through the school gates. It's best that way. Then there's no Knocker to meet on the way home.

It was gone half past four by the time I lifted the catch of the gate and stepped into our back garden. Straight away I heard a voice. It was Tara. I could even see her lips moving in the gap in the fence.

'When did a referee first use a whistle in a football match?' said the lips.

'What?'

'When did a referee first use a whistle in a football match?' she repeated.

'I dunno.'

'1878,' she said.

I took another step towards our back door.

'You been playing football, Sam?'

'Yeah.'

'Are there any girls playing in your team?'

'No.'

'Why not?'

'School rules. No girls.'

'That's stupid rules . . . girls are as good as boys any day.'

I looked at the lips in the gap and then I said, 'I scored a goal today.'

She drew in a sharp breath and then she said, 'You didn't.'

'Did.'

'How'd you do that?' she asked.

'I just ki—'

I stopped in the middle of the word. Could I tell her? Could I really say all about Mika and the sticker and all that? I began to speak again.

'I hit it with . . . '

She didn't let me finish what I wanted to say . . . not choose the right words.

'Did you zap kick it?' she asked.

'Yeah . . . I zap kicked it,' I said and took

another couple of steps towards our back door. My hand was on the door handle.

'Don't go in, Sam,' said Tara loudly.

'Why not?'

'Cos . . . I wanted to warn you . . . she found your blazer.'

My hand came away from the door handle.

'What?' I said. 'How do you know about that?'

'Your mum was shouting about it, right out here. Saying that it was all ripped. "Ruined," she said. I could hear her. She hasn't half got a loud voice your mum.'

I turned to the gap in the fence with the lips showing through.

'I wanted to tell you,' said Tara. 'So you'd know. But your mum has gone out till later. She's gone to take Amber to 'er dancin' lessons. Back about six.'

It went quiet for a bit.

'You can come and wait in my house, Sam, if you like. We could have a game of the football quiz. That one I got for Christmas.'

I didn't go round to Tara's. I just wanted

to be by myself for a bit. What I needed was to try and sort a few things out inside my head. Time to think. I went up to my bedroom.

The blazer was lying on my bed. The patch where the pocket should have been was facing the top. It was all my mother's fault anyway. How could she have put the wrong school badge on that blazer at the beginning? A blue badge with a castle on it instead of the red rose for our school? How could you get them mixed up? But mixed up they were and Knocker and Josh picked on me the very first day I started at that school.

'Look at 'im.'

' 'E's got the wrong badge on 'is blazer.'

'What a thicko.'

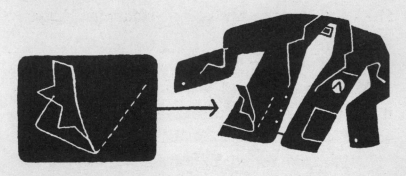

I couldn't touch that blazer on top of my bed. I couldn't go anywhere near it. It came to six o'clock and then half past. Still no sign of Mum or Amber. When they did come in much later they were all happy that Amber had won first prize in a big dance show and the blazer was forgotten for a while.

6

I waited for Knocker to hit next. After I smashed down the goalpost he'd be waiting to pick on me. He was bound to. The next two days it was very quiet. Too quiet.

Then it began. On Monday pages were ripped out of one of my school books. Nobody saw it happen. On Tuesday somebody threw paint all over our front door. Nobody saw it happen. On Wednesday somebody slashed the tyres on my bike. Guess what? Nobody saw it happen.

Thursday was school football. I tried to go sick.

'I can't play, Mr Brailsford.'

'Why not, Sam?'

'Bad leg, sir.'

'Have you got a sick note?'

'No, sir.'

'You know the rules. No sick note, no excuse. Get changed.'

I knew something was going to happen. It did. I turned my back for a few minutes in the changing room and my bag went missing. What was far, far worse was that in the bag were my football shorts and in the shorts pocket was my sticker.

Disaster.

Yes, this was a disaster.

How could I have been so stupid?

'Mr Brailsford . . . my bag is missing.'

'It can't be. Search the changing room.'

'I've searched twice. The bag had— '

'What? What did the bag have in it?'

I paused. I couldn't tell him. No way.

'It had . . . my . . . er . . . football kit in it,' I mumbled.

Mr Brailsford came into the changing room. He looked at all our class.

'Sam's bag has gone missing,' he said. 'Look in all your stuff . . . under the seats . . . in the lockers. Let's see if we can find it.'

The changing room was searched. No bag was found. Mr Brailsford looked at the class.

'No bag, no football lesson,' he said.

'Oh, sir,' said most of the class.

But Mr Brailsford was not shifting.

'If somebody has stolen Sam's bag they are in big trouble. The bag has all his football kit in it. This may be a matter for the police. If one of you here is a thief I want to know who it is.'

It went very quiet. Mr Brailsford was looking at the class.

'I am going to ask you one at a time. Tell me if you know anything about this.'

It was still silent. He spoke to each of us in turn.

'Jamie?'

'No, sir.'

'Ravi?'

'No, sir.'

Mr Brailsford came to face Knocker. He called him by his real name.

'Paul?'

Knocker didn't move at all.

'No, sir,' he said.

I was getting angry. Of course Knocker knew something about it. The slashed tyres, the ripped books, and the wet paint. Oh yes, Mr Big knew plenty about all those. He knew plenty about my missing kit. But did he know about the sticker? If he did I was in real trouble. Only finding out the truth was something else.

Mr Brailsford reached Josh.

'Josh?'

Josh looked down at the ground. He started to bite his lip.

'Josh, do you know something about this?'

Josh mumbled something under his breath.

'What was that?' asked Mr Brailsford.

'No,' said Josh.

'Are you sure?'

Josh bit his lip again. It went very quiet. Then suddenly Charlton jumped up.

'It was Knocker and Josh,' shouted Charlton. 'They did it.'

Now Knocker was angry. 'You liar. I never did anything.'

But Charlton stood his ground. 'They did . . . they did . . . look.'

Charlton pointed up towards the top locker. Everybody's eyes looked up.

'I can't see anything,' said Mr Brailsford.

'They hid his bag on top of the locker. I saw them do it,' said Charlton.

Mr Brailsford climbed up onto a bench. He reached up high and pulled out something. It was covered with cobwebs and dirt. He looked at me.

'Is this your bag, Sam?'

'Yes.'

'Check it over.'

I opened the bag. My boots, shirt, and shorts were inside.

'Is everything OK?' asked Mr Brailsford.

I felt the shorts again. My hand went towards the pockets. Everyone was looking at me. I could feel their eyes staring at me. I daren't let everybody know about the sticker. I pulled my hand back.

'It's OK,' I said.

Mr Brailsford looked straight at Knocker.

'Did you do this?' he asked.

'He did. He did. He's got it in for Sam. Him and Josh,' said Charlton.

'Yes they have. They always pick on him,' shouted the rest of the class.

'Well, they won't any more,' said Mr Brailsford. He looked at Knocker and Josh.

'Get changed out of your kit, you two. No football for you two today.'

They got changed and Mr Brailsford marched them out of the changing room to wait outside his office. Now I was safe. I reached into the pocket of my football shorts. The sticker was still there. I began to breathe more easily again.

I'd won the battle of the football kit thanks to Charlton, but there was still a war going on. A Knocker and Josh war. They wouldn't take any prisoners. They'd show no mercy. I waited for them to strike again. It could be any place and at any time. I had to be on my guard.

Two days later there was a knock on our door. I went to answer it. I opened the door but there was nobody there. I looked up the road both ways. Nobody was in sight.

'A Knocker trick,' I said to myself.

I went to shut the door. Just as I did I saw something on the ground. I went to pick it up. It was an old football shirt that had been cut and ripped and smeared with dirt. Pinned to it was a piece of paper which said:

We are going to get you, Spider.

It wasn't Knocker that struck next but the flu. It hit our school harder than a brick thrown through a window. Kids were sick everywhere. Some puked up in assembly. Some had to be taken home in teachers' cars. Knocker and Josh got it. I couldn't believe my luck. But my luck didn't last. Knocker came back two days later.

I tried to keep cool. I kept my distance from Knocker and went to the library for a bit of shelter. I was hiding behind a big thick book on dinosaurs when Charlton came into the library.

'Sam,' he shouted.

'Quiet please,' said the librarian.

'Guess what?' said Charlton.

'QUIET PLEASE!' shouted the librarian.

Charlton came closer and started to whisper.

'You've been picked.'

'What?' I asked.

'For the school team. Loads of kids are still off sick. So Mr Brailsford said you're in.'

It was true. We both went down to the notice board outside the changing rooms and there it was.

Sam Wicklow, it said in Mr Brailsford's neat handwriting. In a day's time I would be playing my very first match for the under 13s in a cup match against St John's.

Or would I? There was another name written on the team-sheet.

Paul Osborn.

Paul Osborn alias Knocker. I thought of the football shirt thrown at our door. Did I really want to play after all?

Back at home after school Tara was lying in wait.

'How many times have England beaten Germany in the last hundred years, Sam?'

'Dunno, Tara.'

'Yes you do.'

'I said I don't know.'

She glared at me with her spying eye through the gap in the fence.

'I spy with my little eye,' she said.

'I haven't got time for baby games, Tara.'

'Something beginning with "s".'

I tried to ignore her.

'"S" for scared. Who's scared, Sam?' she said.

I stopped walking across the garden.

'You should play, Sam. You've got to play.'

I turned towards the fence.

'What you talking about?'

'Charlton told me all about it,' she said.

I went inside and slammed the door behind me. I wasn't going to let Tara get to me. But I knew in my heart she was right.

It was the day of my first school match. Mr Brailsford was holding a pep talk in the changing room.

'This is the big one,' he said. 'It's a cup match. If we lose we'll be knocked out. It's as simple as that. But we are not going to think of defeat. Oh no. We are going for victory. We're going to win today, aren't we?'

All our voices spoke as one. 'Yes, sir.'

Mr Brailsford looked across our sea of faces.

'Good . . . good,' he said. 'We've made just one team change . . . Sam is a striker. Now all of you remember there are other players in our team besides yourself. Try not to be selfish with the ball. A winning team is a passing team.'

We began to change. Then Mr Brailsford piled a big heap of red and white striped football shirts in the middle of the room.

'New shirts . . . for the match,' he said.

Hands pulled at the pile and soon eager young players poured out of the changing room to begin a pre-match warm up. I was still in the changing room staring at the one shirt that was left. Was that shirt really for me? It was impossible. Knocker was right. I couldn't kick my way out of a bag of chips. I'd better tell Mr Brailsford straight away so he could find a substitute for me. Then Mr Brailsford came into the changing room.

'Come on you, Sam. Get your shirt on,' he said.

'It . . . won't fit,' I lied.

'How do you know . . . you haven't tried it on yet.'

'But, sir, I . . . '

'No buts . . . there isn't time. We're ready to start the match,' he said and went out onto the pitch.

I picked up the new shirt. It felt so sleek and shiny. An idea came to me. The sleeves of the shirt were quite tight. Maybe I could tuck the Mika sticker in the cuff of the sleeve and rub it when I needed a zap kick. That would give me power. I just hoped it wouldn't be power out of control and break the goalposts like last time . . .

'Sam . . . come on, Sam . . . or we shall start without you,' came a cry from outside.

I pulled the shirt on, tucked the sticker inside the sleeve and with my fingers crossed ran out of the changing room and onto the pitch.

In the first half they pounded our defences. Time and time again the ball was crossed with corner after corner but somehow they failed to find the net.

I watched it all from a distance and stood by myself in the centre circle waiting in vain for the ball to come my way. But it never did.

'Get yourself in the game, Sam,' shouted Mr Brailsford from the touchline. 'Go and get the ball . . . don't stand about waiting for it to come to you.'

He was shouting at everybody and beginning to lose his voice. I tried to run but I was scared the sticker would fall out of my sleeve and fall into the mud of the pitch. I just gave up. Then

Knocker had the ball and sped down the pitch like a headless chicken.

'Pass it . . . pass it . . . pass it!' shouted Mr Brailsford. But Knocker held on to it and dribbled away. He cleared one player and a second but he just couldn't stop himself showing off. As usual he tried to dribble it past one opponent too many and lost control of the ball. Our attack broke down and their pounding started all over again.

At last the whistle went for half time and Mr Brailsford gathered us round for what should have been another pep talk. Only we had no pep and he had no voice. So we each sucked half an orange and stood around feeling lost.

The second half began with a freak bit of luck. We caught them napping. From the kick off the ball was booted high up in the air up towards their goal. I forgot about my sticker falling out and sprinted off upfield. There was Knocker by my side running too and a whole gaggle of us charging down the pitch like a lot of sheep being chased by a dog. The ball came down and skidded off one of the St John's defenders for a corner. Our first of the match.

Charlton took the corner, a good one fired just out of reach of their keeper. Up jumped the gaggle. Red and white stripes mingled with yellow. Their heads strained towards the spinning ball. Defenders and attackers struggling desperately to make first contact with the ball.

One tall and sometimes selfish attacker was centimetres higher than the rest. Knocker's head was so close to the ball and an open net beckoned. His head pulled back, poised to strike and missed. Yes, missed the ball completely. The gaggle began to plummet to the earth. Bodies sagged. The ball fell too and struck the chest of Knocker's red and white striped shirt. I could see it spinning in slow motion towards the black mesh of the goal. A goalie's desperate outstretched hand tried to grasp it but the ball was just out of reach. Still spinning it went over the goalie's head and landed firmly in the back of the net.

'Yeees!' shouted Knocker raising his arms aloft, fists clenched and eyes tight shut. We soaked in the triumph. One–nil up. The tide had turned. It was enough to make Mr Brailsford find his voice again.

'Back,' he shouted. 'Back, all of you in defence. Keep it tight. Make them fight for it.'

So back we went and their bombardment started all over again.

Zoom came the ball . . . out went a foot as we cleared the goal line again and again. A big gaggle of bodies bunched in our penalty area. They should have scored loads of goals. But they didn't. Surely it was only a matter of time before they scored. Somebody had to do something. Somebody who had not really played any part in the game and had hardly kicked the ball yet . . . The words Mr Brailsford had said at the start of the match were pounding in my head.

'Wear your shirts with pride.'

It was up to me. It was time for me to show some pride. To stop playing like a scared wimp and show some pride. The next time the ball came anywhere near me I'd do it. Mika wouldn't let me down. My hand was ready on the sticker. Ready to trace round his shape. Ready for him to smile and for me to have the huge power in my leg and crack the ball all the length of the pitch and into their goal. If I kicked from near our goal it would be safe enough not to break the goalposts. Then we'd be two–nil up . . . the game in the bag. Victory was ours for the taking.

They won another corner. This was it. The moment I'd waited for all match. I positioned myself on the goal line, let my finger go round Mika's face as the ball was curving high through the air towards me. My finger was back to the top of the head for the second time and I waited for my leg to go strong and powerful. Only it didn't seem to . . . The ball was almost on me when I began to jump. Up in the air I went, propelled by Mika power. Higher and higher I climbed. I had a sudden panic. Maybe I was going into orbit like the ball in our back garden. Look out, Jupiter . . . here I come.

My arms were hot. Mika power was in my arms. They shot out like a spring uncoiled as I caught the ball just before it hit the back of the net.

'Penalty! Penalty!' screamed the opposition.

I fell to the ground clutching the ball.

'You caught the ball . . . but you're not the goalie,' said a quiet voice. 'You've given away a penalty . . . and now we'll lose the game.'

I heard what they were saying but my legs were out of control. The power had taken over. I was up on my feet clutching the ball at my chest. The ref's whistle was blowing but I took no notice.

'Penalty, Sam,' shouted Mr Brailsford. 'Put the ball down.'

But I didn't. I ran two steps with it. Now everybody was shouting.

'Put the ball down.'

Still I ignored them. I pulled my arm back and hurled the ball forward miles high in the air. As I did so something fell out of the sleeve of my shirt. But I paid no attention to it. I found myself shouting. It was as if I had no control over what I was saying. The words just came out of my mouth by themselves.

'Go on. Go for it. Chase the ball. Let's have a goal. Go for it, Knocker. Go for goal.'

Only Knocker didn't go for goal. Instead he was looking at something on the ground. It was my sticker. It had fallen out of my sleeve. Before I had time to think Knocker bent down and grabbed the sticker in his hand and then crumpled it in his fist.

'Give that back,' I said.

But he wasn't listening.

'You stupid spider. You've ruined our chance of winning the game.' Then he pulled his fist back and punched me in the face.

8

There was blood streaming from my nose. The referee ran towards Knocker at speed. He blew his whistle hard and pulled out a red card.

'Off the field,' he shouted. 'Now.'

Mr Brailsford came running onto the pitch and marched Knocker off towards the changing room. The St John's players began to boo and laugh.

'Off . . . off . . . off,' they chanted.

The referee ran up to me and gave me tissues to wipe away the blood from my nose.

'You better have a sit down,' he said.

'I'm OK,' I said.

It was true. Even though the blood was still pouring out of my nose it didn't seem to hurt at all.

It took ten minutes to restart the game. The

referee placed the ball on the penalty spot. I turned my back. I couldn't watch. It was all my fault and there was nothing I could do about it. It went very quiet. Then I heard feet running along the ground. There was a thud as a foot struck the ball and then a cheer. I didn't need anyone to tell me that St John's had scored.

The ref blew his whistle soon afterwards and we all trooped off the pitch. We got changed in silence. I had thrown away our chance of victory in one stupid moment. The match was a draw. We'd have to have a replay . . .

There was no sign of Knocker. I could see my crumpled sticker in his fist in my mind. I had to get it back off him. But how was I going to do that?

When I got home Tara was waiting. She was up to her usual spying tricks with her nose poked through the gap in our fence.

'What you done to your nose?' she asked.

'Nothing.'

'What you done to your voice?' she asked.

'Nothing.'

'But it's different. It's gone deeper.'

I went into the house and up to my bedroom. Mum and Amber were out as usual. I looked at my face in the mirror to see what damage Knocker's fist had done. There was no blood on my nose but something was strange. My face looked different. It seemed to have grown longer. It was weird. I wondered if it was a trick. Was it Amber messing about? Had she got one of those mirrors like you get in a fairground and put it in my bedroom to scare me?

I ran downstairs to look in another mirror. Different mirror but the same strange face. I began to panic. My heart was racing. Then I remembered concussion. That's what you get when you have a knock on your head and you go all wobbly. Wobbly face means wobbly concussion. That was it. I'd got it sorted. The best thing for concussion was to lie down and take it easy. So that's what I did.

I must have been asleep for ages because when I woke up it was just getting light the next morning. Birds were singing outside the window. It was when I sat up that I first saw them. My legs. Could they be my legs? They had grown. Oh yes, they had grown so that they stuck out nearly to touch my bedroom wall. But it wasn't just my legs that had grown. Oh no. So had my hands. They were huge. My arms and head and chest were ginormous . . . In fact all of me was twice the size it should have been. And there was something else. I looked at the long legs again that seemed to belong to me and saw they were covered in hairs. Thick black hairs also sprouted out of my armpits like a tropical jungle. I had grown a man's body.

As I sat in my bed which was now far too small for me my eyes went towards the mirror on the wall. The same mirror that last night had shown me a long long face. At that moment I knew what had happened. For now I saw not my own face but that of Mika Tailer. By some weird trick I had taken the body of a world famous goalkeeper. It seemed that Mika power had grown so strong it had taken over my whole body. All of me was Mika. There was nothing left of Sam. WOW! Or had I? This couldn't really happen, could it? Was I still suffering from concussion?

I reached into a drawer and pulled out a video. I slotted the video into the TV. Maybe the video could tell me the truth. I looked again in the mirror and back towards the video as it was playing. There could be no mistake. The face in the mirror and the face on the video were exactly the same. Same hair, nose, eyes, mouth. Same man.

'Sam.'

It was my mother's voice.

'Sam!' she shouted. 'Come on, you'll be late for school.'

School? How could I go to school in the body of the world's best goalie? I wouldn't be able to fit my knees under my desk to start with. Trying to pull a boy's ripped blazer over my new body was going to be fun. What would I put on my feet?

'Sam? Are you OK?' asked my mother.

'Yes,' I mumbled trying to make my voice sound normal.

There was a pause. A nasty sort of pause then she asked, 'Are you feeling ill?'

I had to do something about my voice. I pushed my pillow up against my mouth hoping it would sound different and said, 'I'll be out in a minute.'

There was another nasty pause then I could see the bedroom door handle moving.

'Open the door, Sam,' she said.

The door of the bedroom sometimes sticks shut and I just hoped she wouldn't be able to open it. If it did open how was I going to explain to her that her only son had changed into a grown man overnight?

I was saved by Amber.

'Mum, what time is it?' she growled from her bedroom.

'Time you were at school,' said my mother.

'Mum . . . did you wash my PE kit?'

'Yes.'

'Where did you put it?'

'It's downstairs.'

'Mum, could you get it for me?'

I heard my mother grumble and then her footsteps going down the stairs and into the kitchen. I reckon I had less than two minutes. I pushed the bedroom door open and ran down the stairs, taking two steps at a time with ease with my new long legs. On a hook in the hall I saw the long black coat Dad used to wear before he left us. It would be better than walking about in pyjamas that were ten sizes too small for me. I pulled it over my shoulders and tied its belt firmly round my waist. His wellington boots were also in the hall so I slipped my feet into them. Then I could hear my mother coming out of the kitchen still grumbling. I ran to the front door, opened it, stepped through and closed it firmly behind me. With giant strides I stepped out into our back garden.

Tara had started her spy watch early. I caught sight of her face in the gap in the fence. She was staring straight at me with her mouth wide open. It opened and closed like a goldfish's mouth. But I was in no mood for goldfish. By my foot was a football which had got left out days before. I just couldn't resist it. I pulled back my giant foot in the wellington boot. It caught the ball perfectly. The ball zoomed off like a cannon-ball. It hit our gate right in the middle. There was a crunch, a splintering of wood, and the gate fell off its hinges onto the ground. The ball bounced high up into the air and disappeared from sight.

Trying not to look at Tara I stepped out into the street and away from our house. But where was I going? What could I do now?

Out in the street everything seemed to be a bit smaller than usual. I could see right over walls which used to tower above me. The pavement seemed narrower and walking along it was much easier. Perhaps being trapped in a man's body was not so bad after all. People walked past and didn't even notice me. I even put a smile on my face.

In the next street a few kids were waiting for the school bus. I walked casually towards them. Then it started.

'It is,' said one tiny kid.

'Isn't,' said a girl with ginger hair.

'Is,' repeated the tiny kid.

I looked over towards them and stopped. I put a giant smile on my face, held up my giant hand and waved at them.

'Hi,' I said in a deep voice.

'Cor. It is him,' said the ginger girl.

'Go on ask him,' said another kid.

'Ask him what?'

'Ask him if he's Mika Tailer.'

'I'm not. You ask him.'

I smiled and waved my hand again. The ginger girl giggled and then asked, 'Excuse me are you . . . ?'

'Yes,' I said. 'I'm Mika.'

'Paper . . . get his autograph,' said the ginger girl.

'Yeah,' said the tiny kid.

'Yeah,' repeated all the rest of the kids at the bus stop. They all scurried about opening school bags and searching in pockets for pens and paper. A few seconds later the ginger girl thrust a pen and paper towards me. I smiled at her. This was crazy. I was even beginning to think like Mika.

'What's your name?' I asked her.

'Bethany,' she said.

So I wrote

To Bethany
From
Mika

Then I did the same for Ben and Alice and James and Winston. I wrote Mika till my fingers ached. At the end of the queue stood the tiny kid holding open his maths book.

'Can you sign there?' he asked.

'What, in your maths book?'

'Yeah. I've got nothing else for you to write in,' he said.

So I put a big *Mika* at the top of the page and walked off with a spring in my step.

I found my feet taking me towards the street where Knocker lived.

'Yeah. Why not?' I said to myself. 'Why not give him a surprise visit?'

I reckoned that he had to be at home. After punching me like he did Mr Brailsford would have had him suspended from school. Surely he'd be at his house.

I was right. When I got outside Knocker's

house I looked up to the top windows. I could see him through the window playing on his computer. Well, wouldn't he just love to get a visit from a world famous goalkeeper? I stood and watched him for ages and then I saw his mother come out of the side door of the house. She climbed into her car and drove off through the front gates. I watched her go all the way along the road and out of sight. My eyes flicked back towards Knocker. He was in the house alone. I was sure of that. It was a perfect opportunity. For the first time in my life I wasn't afraid of him. If I could now look over brick walls that usually towered miles above my head then surely I could look down at Knocker. For the very first time I was bigger than him. I had bigger legs and arms and feet and bigger fists. I had a bigger brain. Now for the first time I could make him grovel. At last it was his turn to be scared.

I walked calmly across the road. My giant legs strolled through the gates of his house. I raised my huge fist up to knock on the side door. It was at that moment that I saw the side door had been left open. All I had to do was to push the door a little and step inside and make a dream come true.

Yet I hesitated. Could I really do it? I might have a man's body but did I have a man's courage? I could feel those long legs begin to wobble and shake.

'Come on, Sam. You've got to do it. You've got to,' I told myself and with one stride I walked into the house.

I climbed slowly up the stairs of the house. This was spooky. I didn't feel right about being here. I mean, how would I feel if someone did the same to me? But that voice inside me was pulling me on.

I climbed the last stair and stood right outside his bedroom. I could hear the sound of his computer game as he zapped another space-ship of aliens. This was stupid. What was I going to do when I got into his bedroom? Beat him? No way. I'd have to speak to him. But what would I say?

'I'm Mika, I want to talk to you?'

That would be stupid. I took a step back from the door and looked down the stairs. Could I creep away without him knowing that I'd even been there? But what then? I'd be trapped into Mika's body for ever with no way out.

A second later I stepped into his room. I saw the connection from his computer game was in a socket by the door. I reached over to it and snatched the connection out of the socket. Immediately the picture on the computer screen shrank. Then it disappeared altogether as the screen went blank. Knocker swivelled round in his chair and he saw me for the first time. He had the strangest expression on his face that I have ever seen. I took another step into the room.

'Hello, Paul Osborn,' I said.

His face went very white.

'You know who I am,' I said.

'Yes,' he mumbled.

'You've got something of mine,' I said.

He was looking at me like I was a ghost. I had to ask him again.

'You've got something that belongs to me,' I repeated.

'What?' he said.

'You have a sticker of me,' I said.

'What?' he repeated.

I held out my giant hand which he looked at closely.

'Give me that sticker, Paul,' I said.

'Yes,' he said slowly like I had a strange power over him. Then he pulled open a drawer in his computer desk and pulled out a crumpled piece of card.

'Thank you,' I said and opened out my hand to make it even bigger.

He dropped the crumpled card into the palm of my hand. The long fingers of my other hand picked up the crumple. Immediately I could see that it was the Mika sticker. I began to smooth out the crumple further just to make sure. It was so good to touch that sticker once more. In that moment something happened. It began with a tiny tingle in the tip of my finger. The tingle spread to other fingers. It worked its way down my fingers and changed from a tingle into a shock wave which swept over my whole body. I was changing back. Already my hands were no longer Mika's hands but those of a small boy. Soon it would be my arms, legs, and toes. In a few seconds I'd be back to my normal me.

Knocker saw it too.

'Spider,' he shouted. 'Spider, it's you.'

The room was getting bigger and so was Knocker. It was all getting too big for comfort.

No . . . Please . . . Not so soon . . . Let me be Mika for just a bit longer, said a voice in my head.

But it was too late. Before I could stop him he grabbed the sticker out of my hand. Then he ripped it up into tiny pieces and threw them into my face. But he wasn't done yet. He lunged at me with his fist. I ducked just in time.

It was time to make a move. I turned and ran. Being small may have many disadvantages but at least I can move fast when I really need to. My feet touched the top stair and I skipped all the way down them. Up above my head I could hear Knocker lumbering after me. His feet crashed down the stairs. 'Spider . . . Spider,' he shouted.

I ran to the door and leapt outside. I tried to run fast but my feet had grown smaller inside the big wellington boots and my dad's big coat was dragging along the ground. My feet were slipping about and I was slowing down. Then the coat caught on something and I lurched forward and fell to the ground. Knocker could only be a few seconds behind me. I had to think fast. There was no looking back to see how close Knocker was. I pulled my feet out of the boots and my arms out of the coat. Then I ran like I'd never run before. I ran all the way home without stopping and once inside I shut the door tight behind me.

I decided I was through with football. It was too much hassle. Maybe another sport would be safer. The kind of sport where there was no chance of getting trapped into a body that wasn't your own. What about a really boring sport like fishing or dancing? I don't really mind if it is boring as long as it is *safe*.

Even knitting woolly hats seemed appealing so long as the knitting needles didn't get it into their heads to call you a wimp. So that was it then. Football and me were going to be strangers from now on. No football videos or comics. Certainly no stickers. And as for playing football again—well, forget it.

Next day at school I had to go and see Mrs Warren, the headteacher, in her office.

'Come and sit down, Sam,' she said. Then she smiled at me.

'Mr Brailsford came to see me about the football match,' she said. 'I'm very sorry, Sam.'

I looked up at her. Why was she sorry? Was she sorry that the team had drawn when we should have won? Was she sorry that I had picked up the ball and given away a penalty? Why can't adults explain things better?

Perhaps she sensed what was going through my mind.

'I'm sorry about the way Paul Osborn hit you and that you have a black eye,' she said.

'Oh,' I replied.

'We have suspended him from school all week,' she said. 'He won't be coming back until all the bullying is sorted out. I hope you can now relax and enjoy life in school,' she said.

Knocker suspended for a whole week was the best news ever. As for relaxing—well, I don't know about that.

I went back to class in a daze. Charlton offered me some of his sweets. I took three. Ravi said he'd help me with the homework. I gave him my book.

'You can do it for me if you like,' I said.

You never know how long your good luck will last. I went home and tried to watch TV without flicking onto any channels showing football. It was not easy.

My mother's voice called out from downstairs.

'Sam . . . Sam.'

I didn't answer.

'Sam . . . somebody to see you.'

'I'm not in,' I shouted back.

A few minutes later there was a knock on my bedroom door.

'Go away,' I said.

It went quiet and then a small voice said, 'Who said "He can't run, he can't tackle, and he can't head a ball. The only time he goes forward is to toss a coin?" Who said it, Sam?'

'Go away, Tara.'

'It was Tommy Docherty about his captain, Ray Wilkins.'

I said nothing.

'I've come to cheer you up, Sam,' she said.

I still said nothing. Seconds passed. They seemed like hours. Then my bedroom door opened and Tara stepped in.

'How did you get your black eye?' she asked.

I wasn't going to answer that question.

'You got thumped, didn't you? I heard all about it,' she said pulling a football programme out of her pocket.

'I got this for you to look at. I bet you can read it with your good eye. My dad got it. He says he's going to take me to a big Premier match next week . . . and you can come if you like.'

'I've given up football.'

She put the programme into my hands.

'Now you are being daft. You can't give up just like that . . . and anyway that Knocker has been banned.'

'Banned?'

'Yeah. I saw Charlton Harris and he told me.'

I looked at Tara out of my good eye as she sat on a chair near my bedroom window with the sun shining behind her head.

'It all went wrong,' I said.

'What did?' she said.

And I told her. Everything. About the wrong

blazer badge. All about Mika power and the school match. The penalty mix up and me catching the ball. Even getting trapped in Mika's body.

She didn't say anything. She just listened. I thought she might laugh at me when it came to catching the ball. But she didn't. After I'd finished she said, 'It shows one thing, Sam.'

'What?'

'You're a goalie, of course. Not a striker. Never a striker. You should play in goal and then you'll be a really good player.'

I looked at her again. Her voice didn't seem so squeaky now. But more than that I knew she was right.

There was no Knocker at school the next day. His dad had heard about the punch and had taken him up north for a few days to cool him down.

Then it came to the football lesson. Most of the kids just looked at me and said nothing but Charlton said hello. When the two teams were picked I said, 'Can I play in goal, sir?'

'Yes,' said Mr Brailsford with a grin. 'That would be a good idea.'

It was. I had a fair game. Nothing brilliant but I kept a clean sheet and made one decent save. I had no Mika sticker in my pocket and no zap power to call on. But I managed.

That afternoon Charlton Harris came running along the corridor after me.

'Guess what?' he said.

'What?'

'You've been picked again.'

I stared at his ginger-freckled face. Was this some sick joke?

'You've been picked for goalie. Mr Brailsford says you're playing on Wednesday. It's the cup replay.'

I ran along the pavement. I ran past the trees in Lime Grove with their lumbering branches and their outstretched arms ready to trip me up. But I needed to run faster or Goodall's Paper Shop would be closed for the day and then it would be too late. I needed another Mika sticker. If I was going to play again in the school team I had to have the zap power. I couldn't do without it. I knew I could get trapped into Mika's body but I just had to have that sticker.

Into High Street I sprinted just as Mrs Goodall was turning the notice in the window from 'Open' to 'Closed'.

'You've cut it fine,' she said moving off towards the shop counter.

'I ran all the way,' I said trying to get my breath back.

'I can see that,' she said. 'You're all of a lather.'

I didn't know what a lather was but I knew what I had to ask for.

'I was wondering if . . . '

'No,' she said turning off the light above a display cabinet.

'But . . . '

'Sold out.'

She started to take off her referee's black uniform and was ready to hang it on a nail in the wall.

'I need some stickers . . . '

'I said we've sold out. Last lot went ages ago.'

Then she peered closer at me.

'What do you want those for anyway?'

'I . . . I . . .'

'Be snappy,' she said. 'I'm shutting up shop.'

'I want the magic,' I said.

'There's no magic in them,' she said. 'The only real magic you need is in that head of yours.'

'Oh,' I said, not making any sense of what she was saying. Her uniform was hung on the nail and her hand moved towards the light switches for the whole shop. Then it stopped and dipped back into the top pocket of her uniform.

'Still, if it's stickers you want there's just these left,' she said and threw me a small packet just like she had the last time.

'Now take yourself off,' she said. 'I'm ready for my tea.'

Once outside the shop I ripped open the

packet of stickers just like I had last time. But there was something wrong. The first one was blank. It was just a blank white square. So was the second, the third, and the fourth. All white blanks. I turned back towards the shop. The lights were out and the sign said CLOSED in bold print. Mrs Goodall was in the back room having her tea and not even the hammering on the door of a small boy's fists was going to disturb her.

There had to be an answer. I turned the stickers over and over in my hands. I held one up towards my bedroom light to see if anything shone through. I peeled off the backing part to see if they'd been printed the wrong way round and put it on again but there wasn't a letter of writing or scrap of a picture on any of them. I even found an old magnifying glass which had come out of a Christmas cracker but even through that the stickers were blank.

I put them on top of my computer desk, turned on the telly and tried to forget about them. But it was like trying to forget you've got chronic toothache or rotten belly ache. Why had Mrs Goodall wanted to give me blank stickers?

I went over to the computer desk and picked one up again. It seemed to have a tiny dot of black on it like a bit of dirt. I rubbed at it with my finger but the black dot didn't move. I opened my mouth and gave the sticker a big huff with my hot breath and just for a second I did see a faint shape on it. I huffed again and again on all the stickers but nothing appeared.

Maybe I'd dreamed it or something but that faint shape was me. What had Mrs Goodall said?

'The real magic is in your head.'

Somehow I'd just have to manage the football match without Mika. But how? If the magic was in my head then what kind of magic was that? Perhaps she was saying I had to make my own magic . . . out there on the pitch. Wow, this was scary.

I had to be ready for anything . . . that was clear. Ready to leap for the ball in that goal. Ready to throw myself forwards . . . to dive low to the left and right. I had to catch or punch the ball clear if I needed to. More than anything I couldn't be a chicken. If a whole pack of forwards was charging for the goal with the ball at their feet I'd have to dive down and grab it

off them. Then and only then could I be a goalkeeper.

I stood up on my bed and tried to imagine a mob of footballers charging out of the bathroom along the landing past Amber's bedroom heading straight towards me. I got my football and put it on the spot where I thought it might be on the pitch. I began to count aloud.

'One . . . two . . . ' knowing that by the time I got to five I'd have to dive off the bed and get the ball before the forwards did.

'Three . . . four . . . five.'

I dived off the bed, hit the wall with a crash, and crunched my knees on the floor. Mum came running up the stairs and even Amber came out of her bedroom.

'What's going on?' asked Mum.

'I was playing football.'

My mother stared at me.

'You can't play football in your bedroom dressed in your pyjamas, Sam. Now get to sleep.'

Sleep was one thing I couldn't do. The next half an hour was spent bouncing up and down on my bed punching and catching footballs in my goal as quietly as I could. I tried to think how I could get myself out of the house before my mother got up the next morning.

13

They are all going to the school game. Tara and her dad will be there to cheer me.

'I'll keep my fingers crossed the whole game,' said Tara. Even Mum and Amber are going to a football match for the very first time.

'Just so long as the match is over by five o'clock,' said Mum. 'It's Amber's dancing class tonight and we can't be late for that.'

Even as I headed for the changing room a big crowd was pouring onto the field for this last match of the season. It was really going to be something very special. I tried not to think about all those people and just looked straight ahead. I was right by the door of the changing room when who should I see but Knocker hanging around. I thought he was still up north with his dad. No such luck.

But I wasn't going to let him spoil this

special day and walked straight past him and into the changing room. Then the rest of our team came in and so did Mr Brailsford. It was time for another of his pep talks, only he took us off to a classroom for this one and went over what we had to do in the game.

I found it hard to listen to what Mr Brailsford was saying. All I wanted to do was to get changed and get the match over and done with. At last we were back in the changing room and putting on the football strip. I reached into my football shorts pocket to find that blank sticker Mrs Goodall had given me. Even though it was blank I needed its luck. Luck is so important in a big game like this. But I couldn't find the sticker at all. I pulled at the pocket. I turned the pocket inside out and still no sticker. I could feel myself going very red in my face. I went through all my pockets and still no sticker. It must be there somewhere. It had to be. Mr Brailsford came into the room.

'What's wrong, Sam?'

'My football sticker has gone, sir.'

'Check your pockets.'

'I have, sir.'

'Then check your bag.'

'It's a special sticker, sir . . . to bring me luck.'

'What kind of a sticker was it?'

'Erm . . . blank, sir.'

'A blank sticker . . . Sam, this is ridiculous. You don't need a blank sticker. Now get ready. The whistle will be going to start the match.'

My head was in a whirl. I couldn't play without that sticker. I just couldn't. Where had it gone? How had it gone? Nobody would want to steal a blank sticker from the changing rooms . . . nobody would do a thing . . . Yes, they would. They would. If it was a banned kid. A big bully kid who was hanging round the changing rooms . . . he would do it.

'Sam . . . Sam . . . get yourself changed. The match is going to start *any minute!*'

Smack! The ball hits the cross bar. I'm nowhere near it. A few centimetres lower and it would have been in the back of the net. I'm still in a whirl. Jelly legs and heart thumping. My legs won't move. I can't move from the spot. I'm no good at all. There might as well be an empty goal for them to shoot at. I can't stop a flea scoring a goal. This is terrib—Look out . . . look out!

The ball bounces off the cross bar and falls straight at the feet of their big number 9. He charges forward. He's bigger than Knocker. Much bigger. He barges one of our defenders out of the way and then a second. Surely that was a foul, ref. A yellow card at least. But there's no foul given, no whistle blown and on he comes towards me. I suddenly realize there's only me between him and the goal.

I want to crawl away. I'm not up to this. I want to step back and out of his way. Way off on the touchline I see Knocker. He's got my blank sticker. Stolen it. I know he has.

I can hear the breath of their number 9. I've got to do something. Come on, Sam. Come on. Don't be a spider. Not now. I take a step forward and another. I have to narrow his shooting angle. The further I step towards him the narrower the angle and the smaller his target. Keep calm . . . stay on your feet . . . and keep your eye on the ball.

Now he makes a move. The ball is close by his feet. He goes to his right. He wants to dribble the ball past me and lob it into an empty net. No way. It's my turn now. I pounce and dive at his feet . . . Steady . . . steady. If you pull him down it will be a penalty. My hands are on the ball. I pull and tug and the ball comes closer to my chest. Grip it tight. Don't let it go. Just don't.

Ouch! His foot hits me in the stomach. I can't breathe. Then his legs buckle and he falls like an elephant right on top of me.

The ref blows his whistle at last.

'Blinding save, Sam,' shouts somebody but I'm too dazed to know who it is. The world is spinning and reeling. All that I know is that I'm clutching the ball and I mean to keep it. The whistle blows again fiercely this time and Mr Brailsford is running onto the pitch carrying a bag.

'Steady, Sam,' he says and sits me down on the pitch. 'Easy now.' He gives me a drink and looks into my eyes.

'How do you feel?'

'OK.'

Then he takes a cold sponge from his bag and squeezes a load of water down my neck. I start to shiver and he says, 'I think you should go off for a bit. Have a rest.'

'No.'

'But you're shivering.'

'That water was freezing. Let me carry on.'

A few minutes later and I'm back on my feet and back in goal. Charlton takes the goal kick for me and wellies it right down to the far side of the pitch. I take a few deep breaths and the world stops spinning and wobbling about. Then the whistle goes for half time and it's still nil–nil.

Soon after the start of the second half the big number 9 tries a shot at goal again from some distance out. It's a volley right on target and I don't see it until it's right up on me. I'm diving to the left and the ball is going to my right. I try to change direction but it's no good. Somehow the ball strikes the heel of my boot and squirts off across the goal line. If any of their players had been on the spot it would have been a certain goal.

As it is Charlton is there to whack it out for a corner. The goal area is so bunched up I can't see anything.

'Give me some space,' I shout but nobody is listening because the corner kick has already been taken. The ball is zooming towards the goal. It's soaring and lifting right towards the net. I shall have to leap for it. I know I will. Don't jump too soon or you'll miss it by a mile. Steady . . . *now* . . . leap for it *now*. I'm straining my arms and back . . . Somehow I catch the ball. It sticks in both hands firm and true.

'Sam . . . Sam . . . ' shouts Charlton on the wing.

Now is our chance. If I can pass it out to him quick enough we can break from defence to attack in an instant. Yet the pass has to be right to his feet. Only then will the break be on. A kick's no good. I'm no good at kicking. The ball is in my hand and Charlton in my sights. Overarm. It will have to be an overarm throw.

The ball is on its way. It lands right by his feet and Charlton is flying. Yes, he's flying down the wing in masses of space. He clears one defender and then a second. Ryan is in the centre.

'Pass it, Charlton . . . please . . . please pass it,' I scream. But I'm too far away. My voice is lost in the length of the pitch. I can't watch and close my eyes.

'Yeees . . . Goooaall!'

The pass was made and Ryan has scored.

'Goooaall . . . Goooaall!' our chant echoes round the ground. But Mr Brailsford is shouting even louder.

'Concentrate now . . . don't give it away.'

I jolt back to my senses. The few minutes after you've scored a goal is the most likely time you'll give one away. You become sloppy. Inside my gloves I grip my hands tight and jog up and down on my toes.

Somehow we hang on in there. It's still one–nil with just a few minutes to go. Their number 9 has the ball and is heading upfield. I've got him covered. My eyes are on him all the time. As he reaches the edge of the penalty area Josh charges at him and with a huge swathing kick knocks him clean off his feet.

PENALTY! PENALTY! shout the opposition in a loud chorus. The ref blows his whistle with a shrill blast. Josh is given a yellow card and they are given a penalty.

For the first time in the match my hand goes to my pocket. To the place where the sticker of Mika used to be. There's no pocket there now and certainly no sticker.

Now surely the opposition will score and save the match. Our first victory will be no more than a lost dream. Number 9, the team's captain, steps forward and places the ball on the spot. Everyone is quiet now. Out on the touchline Mum and Amber are quiet and so is Tara. Even Knocker is silent. All the players stand still. Number 9 too stands still. He looks at the ball then at the goal and then back at the ball again. He shakes his hands by his sides and then takes three very deliberate steps back. All eyes are on the ball now . . .

Please, Mika, come to my rescue.

He runs forward swiftly and hits the ball hard and true.

Remember the only real magic you need is in your own head.

The ball is right on target and zooms towards the bottom corner of the net. It is perfection. Yet a blurred low shape is moving to the same spot too. A small blurred shape in green is hurling itself towards the ball. Arms fling forward and in a rolling mass of ball and gloves and goalkeeper's body the penalty is saved. The ref blows the final whistle and the under 13s have gained their first victory.

One small goalkeeper is lifted aloft amongst cheers which echo round the ground. Everybody gathers round him. One big boy, once a bully just back from school suspension, stands alone and then walks away by himself.